FlutterByes™

The FlutterBunny™
Thistle

by

Stephen Cosgrove

illustrated by

Diana Rice Bonin

The Nancy Smith Studios, Inc.
Post Office Box 1239
Coeur d'Alene, Idaho 83816-1239

The Nancy Smith Studios, Inc.

Senior Editor: Nancy L. Cosgrove

Creative Editor: Matt Stuart

Design & Layout: Gail Wells-Hess Design Inc.

Senior Curmudgeon: Don Johnston

Keeper of Time: Bob Johnston

Thistle

ISBN Number 0-915396-08-4

Dedicated to Al and Opal Smith.
This story is about roses...and Opal is about roses
and that is more than enough for me.

Stephen

If you followed the glitter of a moonbeam across a starlit sky, you would find a wonderful place called Heaven's Light.

It was here that tiny, winged beings called Earth Angels lived.

Here too lived winged creatures called FlutterByes who flew on whispering winds above the gardens.

There were fuzzy FlutterBears, tiny FlutterMice, purring FlutterCats, and prancing FlutterFly Ponies.

Of all the FlutterByes, the most delightful were the little twitchy-nosed, fuzzy-furred FlutterBunnies. When they were tired, the FlutterBunnies would climb up into the lilac tree and bend their long ears around a branch. Once they were securely fastened, they would simply flop off the branch, swinging right side up. There, they would sleep the night away.

One very special FlutterBunny named Thistle woke every day just as excited as he could be, because he would get to watch the roses grow. To Thistle there was nothing more beautiful than a red velvet rose.

Thistle loved the roses more than anything in the whole wide world. He would hover above the garden and look at the beautiful flowers below. Thistle's fondest wish was to hop in the garden, nose-level with the pretty roses.

But there were rules in Heaven's Light, and one of the biggest rules was that no one was allowed to walk in the rose garden. It was an important rule that was made to protect the delicate roses.

Day after day he would fly above the roses and wish and wish that he could hop below.

It was late one afternoon when Thistle broke this very important rule. He fluttered down to the ground and hopped around under the rose bushes on his big, floppy feet.

"No one will ever know," he whispered as he moved through the blossoms and green leaves. "No one will ever know."

But it was not as wonderful as Thistle thought it would be. For as he hopped, his wings caught on the thorns that protected the roses.

It wasn't much fun at all.

Disappointed, he decided to leave the garden. As he began to fly away he turned to look again at the roses.

"Oh, no!" he cried.

There, scattered on the ground, were hundreds, maybe thousands of rose petals that had been brushed from their thorny stems by his wings.

It was not a pretty sight.

Scared, he flapped his wings even faster, but again they brushed against the roses and even more petals fell to the ground.

Feeling very guilty, he flew back to the bunny tree. He landed with a gentle thump and just sat there for the longest time, worrying about what he had done.

He thought and he thought, "I wish there was something that I could do to fix the roses." But no matter how hard he thought, there was no answer.

In the evening's hush, he quietly climbed up onto the branch of the bunny tree where all the other FlutterBunnies were already asleep.

He carefully wrapped his ears around the branch and flopped over ready to go to sleep.

Unfortunately, there was already a FlutterBunny hanging there. Nose-to-nose, belly-to-belly, they thumped and bumped.

"Oops! Sorry! 'Scuse me!" muttered Thistle.

He tried not to wake the others as he moved farther down the branch. But he accidentally bumped another, who bumped another, and soon all the FlutterBunnies were wide awake.

"Hey, Thistle," a FlutterBunny yawned, "where have you been?"

"Uh, oh, uh, me?" he nervously replied, "I was, uh, walking around on the moon thinking about things and stuff."

Then wrapped in this lie, Thistle fell into a fitful sleep — his head filled with nightmares of the fallen rose petals.

The next morning when he woke, one of the FlutterBunnies said, "You know Thistle, I was playing a game of tickle and hide yesterday on the moon, but I didn't see you there."

"Oh, uh, you wouldn't have seen me because... I uh, saw you hiding there and I flew away so you wouldn't be found," he lied.

Sadly, with every lie he told his ears began to droop from their perky, upright position. Down and down they drooped until they stretched out like an extra pair of fuzzy arms.

Worse was the hurt that he felt in his heart as he tried to cover up the truth about breaking the rule of the garden.

It was later that same day, when Thistle's ears were drooped nearly straight down, that he asked the advice of one of the oldest Earth Angels, Gideon.

"Uh, 'scuse me, Mr. Gideon, sir," he whispered in a small voice, "but I seem to be having a problem with my ears. They won't stay up, they only droop down."

"Hmm," said Gideon wisely, "Things such as ears and wings fall to the ground when they are pulled by a heavy weight. Is there something that is pulling your ears down, a hidden weight you are carrying? Possibly something you feel guilty about?"

"Who, me?" stuttered Thistle. "No, no, I have no weight, no guilt. I, uh, well, I uh..."

Gideon smiled patiently and waited as Thistle's ears drooped lower and lower with every lie he told.

Finally Thistle could take no more. He asked Gideon to come with him so he could show him what he had done. The FlutterBunny put a tiny, fuzzy paw in Gideon's hand, and together they flew to the garden. There, hovering above the ground thickly covered in torn petals, Thistle admitted to breaking the rule.

"Surely," said Thistle in a tiny voice, "my ears are drooped because I broke the rule by walking in the garden of roses."

And sure enough, even as he spoke, his ears began to lift just a tiny bit.

"Yes, little FlutterBunny, breaking the rules weighs heavy on your heart as well as your ears, but there is more."

Two tiny tears trickled down Thistle's cheek. "Worse than landing in the garden and causing the petals to fall from the roses, is that I lied about where I had been in fear of the punishment I would suffer."

"And?" asked Gideon in a gentle voice.

"And I lied about the lies and that led to even more lies. But I am so sorry," he gushed. "I am willing to take my punishment now."

Gideon gently lifted the bunny into his great arms and gave him a loving hug. "Ah, my little FlutterBunny, there is no punishment in Heaven's Light for telling the truth."

And from that day forward, Thistle told only the truth.

Lies are heavy and pull you down;

not telling them is the key.

Remember the lesson that Thistle learned,

and you will always be free.

The Nancy Smith Collection
by Stephen Cosgrove

FlutterByes

illustrated by Diana Rice Bonin

Azalea	Thistle
RoseBud	Daisy

Horses of the Tapestry

illustrated by Loretta Jenkins

Dawn	Nooner
Twilight	Midnight

Earth Angels

illustrated by Kevin McCarthy

Hannah GoBrightly	Plum Pudding
Sarah GoBrightly	Patrick BentWing
Finnigan FireWing	Ruby & Sputters
Jingle Belle	Jacob JingleHinder